Twitching

Light

Alyssa Hazel

to Samantha

Alyssa Hazel

DEDICATION

Pop - For showing love and B-
Movies in equal measure
Natalie - For knowing I could do
better than the first draft.

"What's her superpower?"
"Her writing makes people uncomfortable"

CONTENTS

TESTAMENT

Should they think me mad, show
them my collection of molted angel
feathers. If they consider me crazy
tell them of my quiet
obsession with the color
of water—

And if they should say,
while I'm looking at them through
closed eyelids, *she was quite
bonkers* remind them of ginger
cookies I'd leave for brownies
who lived under my floorboards.

GHOSTS UNDER A WELSH MOON

Ever hear of the Rhai a Gollwyd i'r Tywyllwch? Probably not. Most ghosts aren't popular unless they have a name that's short, sweet, to the point. Ju-On aka the Grudge? Two syllables. And it rolls off the tongue very well. These spirits also have a glamor which the Rhai a Gollwyd i'r Tywyllwch lacks.

The Moon stands as their sole witness now, unless you're foolhardy enough to seek them out. Maybe it's unwise to tell their story. But then again, the fire is

lit, the air is crisp, and the time
is ripe for ghost stories.

Machynys was a larger,
thriving community supported by
coal mining in the nearby
mountains. A happy place, but
simple. Rolling hills and houses
filled with hardworking men and
women. From sunup till sundown, the
men worked the coal mines. They
lived for the few hours they got
with their families after sunset.

One day, a terrible accident
occurred. Some blame faulty
equipment, others blame the
alcoholic overseer, and still
others claim sabotage, but everyone
knows the result. Two hundred men
descended into the mines, but only
five would see the sky again.

Weeks were spent excavating,
but in the end, only ten bodies

were found. Of course, an effort was made to re-open the shaft. Undisturbed ore nestled down there. However, none were willing to enter the mines again. Who would blame them? Consequently, the town evaporated within months.

The land was soon on the market. While the accident scared off most buyers, one company sent a team of five geologists and engineers to examine the area and the mine, to see if it was worth the purchase price. When a few days went by without contact, a search party was dispatched. For days they combed the area, seeking the group who'd camped near the old village.

On the morning of the fourth day, those searching found a gruesome sight. While three seemed to die in a struggle around the fire, their faces stretched into desperate screams, the other two were peaceful in their tents.

Autopsies revealed a thick layer of coal dust inside their lungs.

The rational police community will tell you they must've inhaled the coal dust while investigating a mine. However, if you ask locals who drive by on quiet, moonlit nights, they'll tell you a different story. They'll tell you of the black fog that flows from the mine. Fog that twists and writhes into satires of the human form with occasional sparks of fiery eyes.

If you're lucky, or unlucky, depending on how you view things, they'll direct you to Aeron Hughes. With vapors of alcohol and bitterness on his breath, he'll give you the same story: Wails and pitch fog and red eyes always seeking something.

Give him one more pint and he'll mutter about a doomed childhood excursion.

Aeron and his best friend Elis were dared to spend the night in Machynys. Settling in an abandoned house, they lit a fire to scare off the dark. Around midnight, Aeron got up to relieve himself. He had just finished when the fog began curling from the mine. Paralyzed by terror, he watched it drift closer and closer to where the fire burned.

By the time Aeron found his voice, it was already upon them. If you've gotten to this part of the story, and he hasn't passed out from his own drunkenness, Aeron will look into your eyes. Within them, you'll see cataracts and bad memories.

"Don't carry a light, don't make a noise. That was the mistake Elis made."

JOHN CARPENTER'S *THE THING*

Too bleak. Like good
father's discipline, appreciation
came after decades
misunderstood.

Too gory. Like life's
song and dance. A June bug
on a windshield. A church mouse
by a feline. *Foolish,*

Depressing. A celestial arrived far above
Man. He fought and lost. What
did you think would happen?

VISITORS FROM THE GOBI

I 've been on this table for hours, flat on my back, trying not to move, not to breathe, trying to get my heart to slow its rhythm. The warehouse is dark, but the flickering lights, and my ears, tell me they are still there. To my left, I see Big Fred. His face melted down to the bone.

One of those things, the thing now curled around him and through him, spat at him. There was such a scream on contact. My lips tremble, and I cover it with my hand to muffle the noise. A hiss draws my focus to my other side.

I see what's left of Chen. His real name is Chenghiz, but he said to call him 'Chen'. It's Mongolian. He told me once, during a break a few months back, his grandmother insisted on it. She'd also insisted he be taught the language from the old country. That's why he'd noticed the crate. Olgoi-Khorkhoi, he'd said, laughing. When asked, Chen explained what was so funny.

Apparently, it was the Mongolian version of the Yeti. The "Mongolian Death Worm" was its name stateside. I focused on this information, trying not to break apart as I saw Chen's mouth open. The crimson thing slithered out,

streaked with his blood, antennae
drifting back and forth in the air.

It rose and kept rising until
two feet of its body was exposed.
It seemed to look at me, though it
had no eyes.

I froze. A trapped scream
rattled against my ribs, begging
for release. The worm's head dipped
again, and a wet squelch reached
me. It had begun to eat. I
breathed, letting my body relax as
much as it could.

Being tense won't help me now.
Once my shaking became manageable,
I searched for an escape. I knew
they were blind, and if they
smelled their prey, I would already
be dead.

They probably use vibrations, like those monsters in that film with Kevin Bacon. There was nothing to jump to, and if I ran, they'd be fast enough to catch me. Maybe I could wait them out? I peeked at the window. Vague orange light was smiling through.

The morning shift should be arriving anytime now. Maybe with their help, I could make it. Slowing my breath yet again, my eyes drifted back to Big Fred and Chen. Their own dead gazes, glassy and frigid, splashed anxiety over me. I forced my eyes to the ceiling. A morbid temptation called my eyes to go back, so I squeezed my lids shut. Remaining calm had to be foremost in mind.

I counted backwards from twenty. This became my mantra. Until rattling noise reached my ears. Keys in the side door. A smile crossed my face. The morning shift! They're here! Before I could taste survival, a noise filled me with dread. Hissing. And it came from right below me. I peered over the edge. They were weaving their way, ever so slowly, up the table legs.

RECORD NO. 5 OF THE MYSTERIOUS
BUKLE FISH

Sweat-saturated, and malaria laced I lay
in the bottom of a black
smoke-coughing tug   plowing down

a river whose name
I can't remember   in the fever
fog. The country I can't
pronounce fidgets
and rolls in its slumber. Shrill
birds fluff themselves in my proximity.
      Claims of the Bukle

territory pour
to my ear from the self-proclaimed jaded
Captain. I roll to my side, *What
a crackpot*. Waves

shift the boat again, but I pay
no mind.   *Bukle* goes the cry
from the crew. I curl away. *It must*

be a log. Awed
cries are caught in the   empty
branches above.   My legs

```
stretch to make me see. But
all I catch is a        rainbow
                              tail.
```

Originally Published in Dark River Review

MODO DRACO EST

"I feel for you, pal." Jax took a slow drag from the cigar. The white smoke that exited his great maw circled above his horned head in a pale haze. The dragon was comfortably curled up on his mound of mattresses with a barrel of scotch at one elbow and an empty pizza box at the other. I copied him and let out my own puff of smoke. Then I shifted my position in my worn bean bag chair to a more comfortable one. The corners of my mouth turned down, despite the rich flavor. "And on top of that, the smug brat flipped me the bird as his mom drove off."

"Flipped you the bird?" A scaly brow raised at the colloquialism.

I tried to explain. "It means—"

"Oh, I think I get it. I saw it a couple times on TV," The dragon extended a claw to the 40-inch flat screen attached to a generator.

Looking at the mirrored screen, I finally verbalized the confusion that started when I first became Jax's roommate: "You get satellite in the mountains?"

"When I tilt it right, yeah." Jax nodded, then continued. "You know, for being a human, you're the best roomie I've ever had."

I took a deep gulp of my scotch and pondered the situation. "I guess most of them don't fall through a hole in your roof."

"You'd be surprised." Jax gave a mighty shrug of his shoulder. "I still don't get why your mate got all of your stuff."

"Half and yeah, well, I don't get it either. But it means she doesn't get any more of my money, so that's something." I took another drag. "In the end, this is better than the hovel I got down the mountain."

"I'm sure if you put some paint on it, the place would look better." Jax shifted and stretched.

A gray scale the size of a playing card fell to the ground. The dragon mused over it and sighed. Then he turned back to me. "But I guess you should worry about the whole job situation first."

I leaned back. "Maybe I could pick up a job at that diner."

My ex, Vanessa, had been a sore winner. Not only had she emptied my bank account in the settlement, but she'd also made me empty my desk. Should've known not to take the job her father had offered. My mind longed for relief from the acrid meditations. Taking another drag, I released the foul taste. As the smoke ebbed and curled through the air, I found sanctuary in a memory; a stop on the way to my dad's hunting lodge.

The old neon sign, barely visible through rainy murk, read Pete's Diner. The interior was a worn, but pleasant haven. I could almost smell the full-flavored coffee and feel the soft smile of the woman who'd handed it to me. A better tip than I could afford was left on the smooth wooden table.

"You know I could help you out." Jax rolled onto his back, making the soft earth in the cave shudder for a moment.

I cracked a smile. "Nah, I think I'll figure it out." *First, I need to figure out how to use the washer and dryer, and then I can finally wash my boxers. Three days with the same shorts is probably long enough.*

One scaly brow shot up. "You know, that attitude is what got you here."

A frown crossed my face and I asked, "What do you mean?"

"You let your mate walk all over you. You let your hatchling—what did you call it? Flip you the bird? You got to get a new mindset, man." The dragon focused one ruby basketball-sized eye on me. I could see my tired face reflected in his pupils.

"It's not like I had a choice in the matter," Irritated, I ground the lit end of the cigar into the ashtray.

"Aw, come on man, don't take it out on the cigar! Those things are Cuban!" Jax moaned.

"Sorry." I took a moment then continued. "What should I have done?"

Jax scratched his chest sending three more scales flying. Then he responded. "Not married her in the first place."

"Well that's great advice!" I snapped.

"I mean the woman called herself a 'princess' and went all Bridezilla on her Maid of Honor." Jax dug his claw into the soft earth. "And then there was the whole fact you worked as her assistant at her dad's firm."

"Remind me to never do a drinking game with you again," I muttered.

"It's not my fault you can't hold your liquor," Jax replied.

"I'm not arguing with you there," I glanced back to the hole in the roof I'd fallen through, or Jax's sunroof to be more precise. Or, to be even more precise, the hole I had confessed my worst moments to last week. Apparently, I named it Tim.

I turned back to Jax. "So, what do I do now?"

Jax paused his work and closed his ruby eyes. For the first time in the six months since I'd fallen into his cave, he looked weary.

"Jax?" I set my cigar down and walked over, taking care to avoid the old mattresses he'd piled up to create a pallet.

"Thomas, I'm dying."

For a moment, I didn't say anything. ". . .What?"

He gave a laugh that made dust rain down from the ceiling. "Oh, come on, I'm a dragon! I'm big and loud. You heard me alright."

"I heard you, but, how? Why?"

A snort bubbled from his nose. "Did you think we only died when a man in a tin can drops by with coconuts clacking together?"

"How can you make Monty Python references at a time like this?"

Jax gave me almost an impish look. "I thought you said, 'There is never a time when one shouldn't use a Monty Python reference.'"

How could he be so nonchalant about it?

"I do it because I can," he answered, eyeing my face. A sigh rolled out of him, causing me to stumble back a moment. "Time, my enemy, caught up to me."

It was at that moment I noticed the peeling on his claws and the yellowing of his smoky scales. I sat down in front of him on a chair made of a crate and an old piece of plywood.

"I'm sorry, Jax." I began. "I spent all this time complaining about my ex and my j—"

"Oh, stop that now. It's been nice to complain with someone." With a delicacy that belied his size, Jax set his cigar on a dinner plate that served as his ashtray. A good-humored look settled on giant reptilian face. I fell silent, unsure of what to say, or if I should say anything. The dragon seemed to notice my discomfort, because he hurried on to say something else.

"Don't feel bad. I'm almost three-thousand-years-old, and it's been pretty good if I do say so myself." Jax tilted his head to the side. "But here's the thing. You don't have the time I do. If you want to make the most of those ninety years or so, you need to take my advice."

"What's that?" I lifted my head to look at him.

"Take no crap. Give no crap."

I blinked, confused. Jax picked up the cigar the size of a log and took another puff. "Now where's the remote? I want to try the Netflix you got installed. They put up a new season of my favorite show."

That was the last time Jax talked about his demise. I was never sure if it was because he wanted to put on a brave face, or if he was just indifferent to his own mortality. Instead, he focused on his cigars, his new movie selection, and joking around with me.

"What kind of bagel can fly?"

"Dunno."

"A plain bagel!"

It always sounded better coming from him. Even on the day of his own death, a year later, he still greeted the morning by scaring away squirrels that lived near the den. It was barely two months later, after I refashioned his home into a tomb, that I entered a small cozy coffee shop and looked around for Vanessa. I noticed with more than a little satisfaction that she'd gained weight. As I sat down, I could already see the nasty comments coming to the tip of her tongue.

"You're late." She picked up her phone and flicked over it, ignoring me.

I inwardly grimaced but tried to be civil. "It was difficult to find this pla—"

"What do you want? Are you here to gloat?"

I glanced around and noticed that a few other patrons looked our way. "Gloat?"

"Daddy's firm closed! And it's all your fault!"

My jaw began to tick with irritation. "All I did was open my own firm. I didn't ask—"

Her phone buzzed, and she immediately picked it up. Tempted to roll my eyes, I stopped as I recognized the voice. Our son was yelling over the phone. Yelling at his mother, my ex-wife. I almost felt sorry for her as she visibly winced. Almost. She soon set the phone down and turned to me.

"Well no matter! She screeched. "You'll always be a loser! You hear me? A loser!"

Take no crap. With that, I stood up and left. I walked to the parking lot and slipped into my navy mustang, sliding my new client folders to the passenger side. My eyes stung a little as I put on the dark sunglasses.

Take no crap. I inhaled deeply and then released that foul taste into the air. Then, I shifted into drive and sped down the freeway. I made one stop on the way to my destination, picking out what I needed from the small horde Jax left to me. I set a pack of cigars next to the cave turned mausoleum. The skeleton that would easily tower over a bus almost seemed to

grin in recognition of the brand. I
set one hand on the skull. In the
soft afternoon air, I could almost
see the fangs turn up into a grin.

"Don't smoke them all at once,
okay? You always said—" I sighed
and shook my head. "I'll see you
again soon."

Give no crap.

A half-hour later I arrived at
my destination. The soft bell
jingled as I entered Pete's Diner.
The soft smile greeted me, and the
warm brown eyes sparkled as the
gentle mouth spoke my name.

"Afternoon, Thomas!"

POETRY

Is it easier to catch
smoke wearing gloves? Or are they more
suited for shoving lightning
into bottles and pinning
butterflies on ice sheets
with your bare feet?

But wind-whisper wings still
twitch light. Sparks and
incense will float over altars.

JUST ANOTHER TUESDAY

Having an insurance agent, the word *fraud* on his lips, show up to ones workplace is never a good sign. Having an internal affairs agent appear is a real omen of doom. When both showed up asking for Martin Hare and Stewart Burke at the end of a very long day on the job, Marty and Stew both knew they had a long explanation before them. Surrounded by opposition, empty Styrofoam cups, and August humidity, Stew and Marty began their story about how the man they were sent to resurrect turned into a zombie.

Little ceremony had accompanied the necromancers as they strode through the funeral parlor. In fact, their arrival received more glares than anything else. Though threadbare carpeting muffled their entry, service goers were alerted by squeaking wheels. Incensed eyes peeked through the privacy curtain as the duo went where most eventually go— the mortuary.

A freelance necromancer at a funeral wasn't odd. When the corpse was intact, it was common practice for there to be one last look over the body. Not to check for revivability— chemicals had long since nulled that option. No, if

the deceased had felt generous, or
their family was vindictive, the
body would be donated to a local
university or some sorcerer in need
of test subjects. If this was the
case, a necromancer would accompany
the corpse to the graveside.
Following mourning, the casket
would descend empty.

No, eyebrows raised with the
appearance of a patch both
necromancers wore on their left
shoulder. It was dark blue circle
with a minimalist white skull
embroidered in the middle. It was
the symbol of the Emergency
Necromancy Service. Someone had
died before their time.

Before they'd even reached
Jackson and Sons Funeral Home,

Marty noted to Stew that this was a weird call.

"What do you mean?" Stew responded around a bite of ham sandwich. Though the rookie was well past his certification program his voice seemed stuck at puberty's beginning. Combined with his baby face and sprinkled acne, Marty had thought him still in high school.

"Fifty-two," Marty snarked.

Stew swallowed and frowned. "Sorry?"

"Fifty-two times I've had to resurrect people who talked with their mouth full." Marty flicked his blinker. "Don't lose your paycheck for a dumb reason."

"Oh."

"Yeah, so, apparently this job we're doing is on credit."

"We're doing a revive on credit?" Stew grabbed his sandwich's second half. A squirt of Dijon landed on his lapel. Vague disappointment coated his next words.

"I thought that was against company policy."

"Normally, it is. But Jackson is—was, tight with Tatsu." Marty made a left turn. "A lot of referrals. Funeral home recommends us, and they get a cut if we get customers."

When Stew didn't say anything in response, Marty continued.

"Our guy, Jackson, he may've been murdered."

"Murdered!" Stewart yelled, eyes wide.

"Don't yell in my ear," Marty snapped. "It's my good ear."

"Sorry. Shouldn't the police be called?"

A red light faded into view. The older man gently settled on the brakes, then turned to his colleague. "What would you rather have? A dead body to investigate or a live person who can tell you who killed them?"

Stew pursed his lips and then responded. "A live person."

"The police agree. At least in this state."

Upon arriving, they were greeted by a squirrel of an older woman in a worn black pantsuit. She waved them to a side hallway, her eyes twitching over to the service area. Goal in sight, Marty and Stew quickened their pace. The gurney's squeak soon peppered the air. With every rotation, the old woman's nose wrinkled with displeasure. Time slowed to an agonizing crawl. When they arrived, she didn't bother with niceties.

Adjusting her gold-rimmed glasses, she leaned in and whispered, "He's in the mortuary."

There was a casual, yet solemn air to their short journey. The directions they received were followed to the letter. Go to the hall's end. Enter the air lock room. Descend in an ancient freight elevator. Flick the first switch and not the second when entering the basement. *For the love of all that's holy, don't flick the second switch.*

Go down the final hallway. Don't look inside any doors but the one at the end. And if you do, don't scream.

Marty rolled his eyes at this final comment. "This isn't my first time going down there, Nancy."

"And you left us quite a mess last time, Martin."

Goosebumps emerged as the temperature dropped twenty degrees. Any skitters, flickers, or rustles to their sides were ignored. A whimpering from an entry near the

end made Stew pause, but Marty
pushed him on with a somber
explanation:

"It takes some work to make
them rest in peace, ya know."

A few feet away from their
destination they stopped. One last
squeak from the gurney rattled the
atmosphere. Before them was a metal
door, peeling from age. On it was a
sign. A single word was etched
there: *Morgue.*

Reaching under the gurney,
both men grabbed their supplies.
Utility belts went over coveralls.
Arcane focuses were hung around
their necks. Latex gloves and
goggles were snapped on. Stew
grimaced when he discovered his
boot covers were missing.

"These are new shoes."

"Sorry princess, I ain't lending you mine. Remember your full suit up next time." Marty reached toward the doorknob. Turning slowly, he pushed the door inwards. Light from the hall trickled on to three stainless steel slabs. Laying on the middle one was a familiar silhouette. A short fumbling later, a switch was found. Clinical light fell over a corpse.

But not the one they'd come to get. A little old lady, with hair like blue cotton candy, gazed up at the ceiling. While Marty moved further in, Stew took a glance at her toe tag.

"Jacqueline Graham," He turned to Marty. "I hope her burial isn't postponed. This being a crime scene and all."

"She's not going to be late for another appointment. Believe me, wherever she ended up, she's got all the time in the world." For a moment it seemed Marty was going to say something else, but his posture stiffened.

"What is it?"

"Our guy," Marty waved him over.

It was Mr. Jackson, of Jackson and Sons. He was a tall man, shaved bald, covered with a thin sheet of ice. Marty kneeled next to the corpse. After a brief examination, the older man swore under his breath.

"Freakin'—Why couldn't they've just stabbed the guy?" Marty looked around the room. "Bunsen burner? No. Stew?"

"Yeah?"

"Got a lighter?"

"No. That's not standard equipment, your Highness." Stew snarked.

"Didn't they teach you better retorts in college?" Marty rolled his eyes. "We've got to take him back to the office. Got to thaw him."

Stew frowned. "Couldn't we resurrect him now?"

"Yeah, if you want him frozen when he wakes up."

Stew nodded. "Alright. Got it. I'll get the feet."

Together, they strapped Jackson onto the gurney. As the last buckle clicked into place, Stew frowned and rubbed his upper arms.

"Did it get—" as he spoke, vapor curled from his mouth, "—colder?"

Marty nodded, a worried grumble on the older man's lips. His eyes shifted around and stopped above Stew's head. Marty's eyes lit up. Turning, Stew saw what caused the change. A half-sphere, covered in spider webs, was embedded in the wall. A warped, mother-of-pearl tinged image reflected in its convex surface. There was a complex, mystical name for this surveillance device but most had a simpler name for it.

"A big scryer?" A relieved smile grew across Stew's face. "If we can get to the source—"

"We can see who did it."

Without another word, they rolled Jackson towards the elevator. The chill was now obvious. Teeth rattled. Hands shook. Marty slammed his palm into the call button. A clank and a tremble signaled the elevator's start up. A screech signaled its stop. Soft moans from the side doors behind them reigned in the silence.

"Ah, crap." Foreboding gripped Stewart. "Know any mechanism magic?"

"Nope. Necro through and through." Marty's grip on the gurney grew white knuckled. "See any stairs?"

It was Stew's turn to shake his head. "Fire marshal would have a field day with this place."

"Check around. There has to be something—" Eyes lighting up, Stewart darted to a red box emblazoned with the words: *In Case of Emergency*. Popping open the lid, he dug through the contents.

Marty breathed into his hands, his eyes going to the corpse. "Finding anything Stew?"

The younger man ran back over. Holy water sat in one hand, in the other was a foot-tall iron crucifix and a stake. "I was looking for a fire axe but…hopefully the crucifix will work?"

Taking the iron piece from him, Marty jammed the narrow end into the crack in the elevator doors. After some finagling, the tip found a foothold. Gritting his teeth, Marty pushed. The doors creaked but nothing gave. At any other time, Stew would've laughed. Losing feeling in one's toes, however, took any humor from the situation. Marty pushed again, this time with Stew's help. Their situation did not change.

Stew was barely able to keep Marty from flinging the crucifix into the wall.

"That's not going to help!" Stew reminded.

"Well, I would take any suggestions!"

"We just need a little more weight put into it."

Rage easing, a spark emerged in Marty's eye. "There's about two hundred pounds right here."

***

Marty looked at Stew. "You were the one who suggested we raise the guy, not me."

"Oh, so I suppose we should've just thrown the body at the door?" Stew retaliated.

The insurance representative had thankfully gone to speak to their superior twenty minutes after he'd arrived. Unfortunately, the internal affairs agent, a Mrs. Graham, hadn't gone that route. She'd been grilling them for over two hours now, and the room's temperature had reflected this hostility. Dark, damp circles had formed in both men's armpits, but Mrs. Graham's cool and composed exterior suggested she could do this all night.

She folded her hands on the table and looked them dead in the eye. "I don't care *who* suggested it. What I do care about is how,

following your escape, you managed
to let Mr. Jackson *eat* a person!"

She pointed behind them and on
instinct they looked back. The
revitalized Mr. Jackson, skin blue
and eyes red, paused his current
preoccupation— ramming himself into
the wall— just long enough to
return their gaze. Standard
procedures said zombies were
supposed to be held in a shark
cage. With the only spare one with
the maintenance crew, a collar and
chain was the next best thing. It
had worked fairly well. Except for
when Jackson had swiped at Mrs.
Graham.

"Uh, Mrs. Graham." Stew
swallowed; his mouth dry. "We
didn't exactly *let* him."

Marty chimed in at this point. "He charged her the second we got out of the elevator. She probably murdered him. This was retaliation. That'll go on our official report—"

"It will. But both of you gentlemen won't be here to see it filed. You two are—"

"You didn't let me finish." Marty interrupted. "It'll go on our official report *if* I get a generous retirement package and Stew here gets a raise."

A groan began to fill the room as Jackson shuffled toward them. Though stopped by the cage, the dead man kept pushing against the bars.

"Now why should I give anything to either of you?" A nervous strain permeated her voice.

"Because you don't want it to get out that you murdered Mr. Jackson."

". . .What a ridiculous claim."

"Ridiculous? Maybe. True? Yes."

"You should've cleared out those big scryers more thoroughly," Stew added with a grin.

A hiss bubbled from between Graham's teeth. "How do I know that you won't tell someone?"

"You don't." Marty stood and clapped his hand on Stew's shoulder. "So, keep Stew happy and my retirement checks coming. Got it?"

Graham didn't speak but nodded.

"Good. We'll be going now." Marty waved. "We'll hear from you soon."

A cool breeze swept them as the main entrance slammed shut behind the duo. The last tongues of orange twilight licked the night sky and small insects danced around the security lights. Stew turned to Marty. Eyes wide, he asked: "How did you know?"

"She didn't sweat." Marty shrugged.

Stew stopped on the sidewalk and waited for more insights. When it was clear there was none, he dashed to catch up with Marty.

"Are you freakin' kidding me? You accused her over sweat?"

"Only an ice witch could stay cool in that oven."

"But you—"

"Besides. She was about to fire me. Nothing left to lose after that."

"But—"

"I suppose she also knew about our 'zombie incident' too fast. We hadn't even gotten back before she knew."

"But—"

"You know any words besides 'but'?"

Stew stopped and took a deep breath. "What do I do now?"

"What do you mean?"

"Go home, go to sleep, be here tomorrow. Get your raise."

"But I'd be working with a murderer."

"There are worse coworkers, believe me."

A rebuttal almost made its way out of Stew's mouth until he realized Marty had a point.

"I guess this is goodbye?"

"I guess it is." Marty set his hand on Stew's shoulder. "I'll see you around."

"Sure." Stew smiled. Something curled in the back of his mind. A half-baked memory revolved around his conscious. "Aren't we forgetting something?"

Screams, along with those making them, poured from the building. Stew and Marty recognized them as office workers, non-necros. Stumbling behind them were two zombies: Jackson and Mrs. Graham. Both men went to their work van and opened the back. Besides the gurney, there stood their yew clubs, ketch-all poles and holy water.

"Guess I'm not retiring." Marty sighed.

"At least we get overtime."

STRESS FRACTURES

Bones become dust before the body
turns when eyes swell into

crust. I wait for water to stop
without turning the faucet.
Martha/Love,

when you are too young to feel
this old, sensation consists of
pops,

creaks, and groans of tendons,
joints,
and gray matters.

TICKS

There was always a slight tapping this time of night, and when I mean this time, I mean this exact time: 2:05 AM. When I was younger, I heard a story from my grandmother about goblins who burrowed deep in the earth like rabbits. The rascals would come from under the earth and eat children who stayed up past their bedtime. I suspect, looking back at it now, she thought I was of brave stock.

After all, Grandpa was nicknamed Tarzan after his physical

prowess and love of nature, and Grandma had killed a grizzly in her younger years. It now lived with them as a rug near the great fireplace.

That tapping keeps me awake now. Rat tatt, rat tatt tatt. It will go on for about fifteen minutes before stopping. I've timed it. Rat tatt, rat tatt tatt. We never did figure out what caused the sound. It could've been trees, but there were none near my windows. It could've been squirrels, but several exterminators revealed none within the walls. We'd moved several times. Once when Dad had to go to Tennessee for work, then back from Tennessee when my parents were no longer "compatible."

Rat tatt, rat tatt tatt. I guess even now, fifteen years after I left my home I'm still drawing squirrels. I glance to my roommate. Her breathing is barely perceptible. She's got asthma or some crap like that to do with her lungs. Maybe I should call for a doctor or something, but she'd probably yell at me again just like she always does when she's on her "prescription." Rat tatt, rat tatt tatt.

I got up, just like I'd done most nights for the past twenty years and went over to the window. No trees were even on this side of the housing, the university planners preferring low maintenance grass and concrete rather than anything pleasing to the eye. I spotted a small bird, a canary from what I could tell in the low light. Hoping for a moment telepathy was actually real, I pushed my thoughts toward the little bird.

Hey, you. Are you keeping me up?

The bird glanced at me. It twitched its head one way, then another, then flew away.

Well, screw you too.

I glanced around again, hoping to find the source, when I heard it again. Rat tatt. I glanced at the clock. 2:15 AM. Only five more minutes until it was over. I got back under the covers. Maybe Mom was right. Maybe I should see a doctor about it. Could just be something rattling around up there.

Some duct tape and a glitter
sticker put on my skull and it
would look like brand new. But what
if it was something that needed
more than a quick fix?

Grandma had lied of course in
those later years, but not through
her own intent. Grandpa had hated
the outdoors, as Dad would tell me
later. Rat tatt, Rat tatt tatt.
Though Dad was now on
"prescriptions" himself. Rat tatt,
Rat tatt tatt. I pulled the blanket
up to my chin.

It's just a little noise.
Nothing to worry about.

Rat tatt, Rat tatt tatt.

I closed my eyes, then
reopened them. 2:17. Rat tatt, Rat
tatt tatt. Just three more minutes,

and then I could rest. Two more
minutes and I could forget this
even happens. At least until 2:05
AM the next day. Rat tatt, rat tatt
tatt.

It's nothing to worry about.
There's no monster, only noise.
Noise can't hurt me. Rat tatt, rat
tatt tatt. Breathe in, breathe out.
Breathe in, breathe out. Rat tatt,
rat tatt tatt. I can feel my eyes
grow moist and my breath catch.
Count it out.

One….Two…Three…Four…

Rat tatt, rat tatt tatt.

2:19 AM. Sixty seconds. That's
all I need to last. Just count them
out. Just count them out.

Forty-nine, forty-eight,
forty-seven, forty-six-

Rat tatt, rat tatt tatt.

Thirty-eight, thirty-seven,
thirty-six, thirty-fiv-

Rat tatt, rat tatt tatt. rat
tatt, rat tatt tatt. rat tatt, rat
tatt tatt.

Twenty-seven, twenty-six,
twenty-five, twenty-four, twenty-
three-

Rat tatt, rat tatt tatt. rat
tatt, rat tatt tatt.

Fifteen, fourteen, thirteen,
twelve, eleven, te-

Rat tatt, rat tatt tatt. rat
tatt, rat tatt tatt.

Five, four, three, two, one.

2:19 AM

Rat tatt, Rat tatt tatt. Rat tatt, Rat tatt tatt. Rat tatt, Rat tatt tatt.

The clock is broken.

9 AM greeted me like a sledgehammer to the face. I stood and walked towards the clock. Its digital countenance stared blankly back as I unplugged it and tucked it under my arm. Padding towards the door on the worn, default grey carpet, I met my roommate's gaze. She sipped her coffee, shrugged, and looked back at her laptop.

It was cold outside, but I moved slowly towards the dumpsters. With a little bit of ceremony, I lifted the lid and gingerly set in the clock. I lowered the lid. All I

could do is listen. And it said
nothing. And in the silence of that
following day I realized how lonely
it was

THE SANDMAN (1991)

Tapping the drum never staved night,
but you tried. When two hands reached   toward   eight o'
clock. Mother pulled
          a string through a hoop. A gaunt man
                    from the coffin swung a bell,

signaling
ascent from orange safety
                              to cerulean gauntlet. You listen

to moaning, creaking, two crashes. One
the door, second the window—three the cold
coalescence between face and waning

          moon. Lights: silver and gold beneath   upper and lower
openings. Tap
lower twice— Intoxicated   by the notion Mother
received

          a warning, but still she can't give   sanctuary
from the raven/man who throws fool's dust to get   eyes wide
open— Before he tears them
                    out to fill his children's stomach. He is a good father—

THE MAN WITH THE STICK

The first time I saw the man with the stick, I was at the local soup kitchen. It was around Christmas time, and my family and I decided to put in some volunteer hours.

It was the season of giving after all. So, there we were: My husband DaShawn, my kid Benji, and my mother-in-law Vicky.

A crick and a headache were sprouting from me, but all of us were exhausted, greasy, with our faces tired from smiling. Don't get me wrong, we were happy to volunteer. And the first hour went fine. But helping at a soup kitchen

is a lot different from what you
see in the movies and on
television.

Those in line were far from
airbrushed. Several times people
complained their food wasn't hot
enough, and one guy threw up on the
floor. DaShawn, good guy that he
is, cleaned it up. In passing, he
whispered to me with a mischievous
tone: "Don't wrinkle your nose.
Benji had colic at least three
times."

I rolled my eyes and muttered
back, "Five."

Things didn't get better after
the second hour. A couple of people
eyed Benji in a way which freaked
me out, so I had Vicky take him
home. He wasn't little; his twelfth
birthday was two weeks ago. He
wasn't reckless or the type to

wander off with strangers, but still, my momma instincts wanted him safe at home. About twenty minutes before DaShawn and I were supposed to check out, *he* walked in. At first glance, he seemed harmless enough, except for the stick he carried. In a way, he resembled the stick— hardened, lean, with a leathery quality to his skin. He was probably five-eight, a head shorter than DaShawn, but something about him made me glad I sent Benji home.

Apparently, I wasn't the only one who shared this sentiment. Three other patrons left as the man strode farther inside. As he grew closer, I picked out more features. With each one I gathered, I grew more and more anxious.

His eyes were deep-set and shark-like, and he moved in an odd way. Like he could change direction suddenly, without missing a beat. An insect wriggled through his matted beard. I clamped down on the urge to vomit and touched DaShawn's hand with my own. How the old man noticed this action, I don't know. Our hands were behind the counter. But the moment our fingers intertwined, he reacted.

Looking at me, his head tilted. He turned, moving with weird speed to the side of the room. Then, with an exaggerated slowness, he set the stick against the wall. Exhibition done, he moved back toward the counter.

DaShawn acknowledged my gesture with a squeeze, but still smiled and greeted the new arrival.

No response was given except for a long slow grin in my direction. The few teeth remaining were yellowed stubs within inflamed gums. From behind us, the volunteer coordinator snapped at the old man.

"Bruce! Leave those nice people alone and eat your dinner. There are people waitin' behind you." Her eyes burned into him.

Begrudgingly, the old man frowned, took his plate and moved on. I relaxed and focused on finishing the shift. The coordinator explained 'Bruce' was a regular. He never did anything violent, but he wasn't someone they encouraged to stay long. As she explained, I felt eyes drill into my back. I turned. Like a swine, Bruce rooted through his food.

Mashed potatoes were smeared across his face.

When he noticed I was looking back, he picked up a previously discarded chicken bone and bit down on the middle. It snapped. I shuddered and counted the minutes until we could leave.

Thankfully, Bruce was gone by the time Dashawn and I were finished. He'd given me one more glance before he left. However, this time Dashawn had politely, but firmly, walked him out. I wished I could've said it was over at this point. But upon leaving the kitchen, we saw an omen of what was yet to come.

A flickering streetlight revealed the carcass of our car. Every window was shattered. The front hood and passenger door were caved in, and each of the four tires had a gaping hole. As Dashawn looked it over, cursing and pulling out his phone to call the police, I noticed a crow—maybe a raven—perched on the top of the vehicle. It defecated, tilted its head at me, then flew off into the night.

The second time I saw the man with the stick was in early spring. It was pouring, and I'd gotten the call that Benji's soccer practice was cancelled. My jacket did little as the rain battered me on my way to the car. I'd forgotten about Bruce, except for when I looked at our newish van. As I opened the driver's side, something caused the hair on the back of my neck to stand up. A bird's call, somehow breaking through the rain's violent cries.

I peeked back and sitting on
my front porch was a crow. It took
off. I jumped into the car and
hurried to start the ignition when
I realized it was flying in the
direction of Benji's school. I'm
not exactly proud of how I drove
during those next fifteen minutes,
but in that moment, I didn't care.
Especially when I started seeing
Bruce, along the way.

A silhouette drenched in rain,
but still smiling. At first I
thought I was seeing things, but
after the second time and the
third, I knew I had to get there in
time to save Benji. From what, I
didn't know.

The instant I parked, I leapt
from the car, leaving the keys in
the ignition. Within a few minutes
I was in the office, gasping and

squeezing Benji in a hug. I could hear the receptionist ask if everything was alright, and I muttered, "I'm fine. I'm fine."

Trying to shield Benji from what could be outside, I peered through the glass front door. My eyes widened. There he stood, stick in one hand, and something else in the other. It was a mug, one from my car. Script decorated the ceramic, but I didn't need to be close to know what it said. *World's Best Mom.* A gift from last Mother's Day. Benji called from behind me, asking who he was. I turned to answer but didn't know what to say. The man called Bruce was gone by the time I turned back.

After this last incident, I wasn't sure what to do. DaShawn and I went to the police to file a

report, but I knew there wasn't
much they could do. They could
search for him, but then they'd
looked for him after our car was
smashed up. Benji's school was told
to keep an eye out for the man,
since he'd been trespassing. My
initial thought was to transfer
Benji, but I was reminded he had
only a month or two left anyways.
He'd be heading to high school
then.

DaShawn and I found a
compromise in Lilah, a German
Shepard. She was a rescue, and
after a few months we had her
trained and ready to be our
official guard dog. And for a
while, everything seemed quiet.

Four years of life passed.
Dashawn and I grew grayer through
skateboard accidents, plummeting

GPAs, garage bands, and trashy girlfriends. But we also grew prouder in the late study nights, well-earned A's, volunteer hours, and a sweetheart named Naomi. Benji brought up college a few times, but eventually decided to go into a trade.

All was good. All was still. Then came the camping trip. To celebrate graduation, DaShawn, and Benji decided to head out to the nearby woods for the weekend. I wasn't exactly thrilled, not being the outdoorsy type, but the day before found me curled up next to the toilet bowl. I told them I'd be fine, to go on without me. With a smile I turned Benji's blue baseball cap forward and told him to use toilet paper instead of leaves, referencing a previous incident with poison ivy. Finally, I hugged and kissed DaShawn.

"Come home safe."

The second morning after I saw them off, I woke up to see Benji's blue baseball cap on my nightstand. At first, I worried one of them had sprained their neck and they'd come home early. The scent of coffee drifting up from downstairs supported this notion. I pulled on my bathrobe and went downstairs, ready to tell them it was dumb to leap into a lake from a hundred feet up or try to climb to the top of some scrawny tree. No one was in the kitchen though. Just a cup of coffee. I saw this as a potential peace offering. I grasped the handle only to drop it on the floor. It shattered. But not before

I read the words on it. *World's Best Mom.*

He was in my house.

I grabbed my phone and ran to the door. My hand had just curled around the handle when the butt of a staff slammed into it. I turned. Victory danced in his eyes just as he swung the stick into my head. My body dragged over cold tile as the world faded away.

I woke up in our basement. The air, usually smelling of detergent, was drenched in decay and rot. I tried to move my arms, but they were bound with strong cord. Any attempt to stay calm vaporized when I saw who sat across from me. Benji. If he was alive or dead, I couldn't tell. There was no response when I called his name. Sitting on the washer was a crow.

It peered at me, turning its head back and forth. Tears pricked but I shook them off. I needed to think.

A hand settled on my chair's back. It was him. There was something different about him, Bruce, whatever he was. He skin seemed waxen, and paper thin. The overhead light's glow made him appear translucent. He stood, back to me, and stared at Benji. I found my voice.

"Your-your name is Bruce, right? Look, I don't have a lot of money, but I—"

He set his hand on Benji's hair. I lost it, calling him every name I knew, and others I made up on the spot. But he only lost his concentration when I asked him a question.

"Why us?"

He shrugged. Then, something happened. Something which, on the rare nights I get to sleep without aid, infects my dreams. He grinned, wider than he'd ever done before.

Yellowed teeth rained down onto the floor. Two cracks formed on either side of his mouth and kept growing. A blackened, forked tongue swept his lips and shot forward, pulling a reptilian snout through. Soon the cracks reached down the side of the man's neck. Skin rolled down like a banana's peel, revealing a being which was like a snake, but constructed from gray smoke and dark red ichor.

It worked quickly, constricting around Benji's torso. As it squeezed, there was no cracking bones or breath leaving the lungs. Instead the creature

grew smaller and smaller, allowing
itself to be absorbed into this new
flesh. Soon it was gone.

"Benji?" The name warbled from
my mouth.

My son's head snapped up. He
stood, like a marionette puppet
adjusting to life without strings.
Stretching, he ignored my cries and
curses. Joints popped and crackled.
He whistled, and the crow jumped to
his shoulder. He went to leave, and
I prayed he would just go. His foot
hit the first step and he paused.
Turning he came back over to me. I
set my shoulders back, prepared,
but he instead picked up his stick.
He tested his weight against it,
thoroughly enjoying himself.

"I hope you choke on it," I
muttered.

He opened his mouth, as if to laugh, but stopped himself. His tongue flicked out, as he stared at me, pondering something. There was a cruelty in his eyes which refreshed my anger. Those were Benji's eyes. He grinned and reached toward me. I struggled against the ropes, trying to get the leverage to kick him or hit him. There was nothing I could do. He touched my stomach, and his grin grew again.

I didn't know I could feel dread worse than before, but now I reached a new level. He then did something surprising. He spoke.

"Well, this has been fun Susan. Let's do this again."

After one more glance at my stomach, he went up the basement stairs. He must've left the front door open, because the police found me a few hours later. I was on my side, numb from trying to wrench myself free. And from everything else.

I learned several things over those next few days. First, DaShawn was found dead in the woods next to the campsite. His mother and I barely kept it together. The second news kept us afloat.

I was five weeks pregnant. There was something both wonderful and terrible in this news. New life, but that thing with Benji's face kept coming to mind. Finally, I learned the identity of the old man. His name really was Bruce. Bruce Sodenson. My great-grandfather.

My baby arrived a week ago.
The crow arrived this morning.

MORPH(EUS/INE)

NASA paid a thousand a day to watch
someone rest. Did they have
a degree? I bet

this hypothetical piece
of paper gave no idea
how to fill out

a W2. Don't leave
the program. Waste
your money/time on learning how

to make a poncho. You can't form a
stitch
final semester. Did Mister Sandman
sell you
the dust falling through your
fingers? Why didn't

you clean him
out of his snake oil supply?
Passion

didn't need shackles to keep

you here. The door is open. Drive
doesn't stalk skill. Reality
TV is earnest in this one

regard. Live your dreams
and you'll end half-way through.

I thought he was from the
Chordettes
not Metallica

HERXHEIMERS

I thought the medicine would help me. It had been three months since I'd begun taking those little yellow pills and all I'd gained were night sweats, fever dreams, aches, spiking pain, nausea, and grogginess I could never shake. In all of this, I did not dream.

My grip was white-knuckled on the wheel as I tried to ease my way down the driveway. Lids closing for a moment, I was shaken by a yelp from my back-seat. I slammed my foot on the brake just before my front bumper crunched into a tree.

Chest heaving, I parked. Sweat tickled my forehead. I turned to the backseat, swallowing a few times before speaking to the passenger.

"Hey Jaden. I-I don't think I can drive you to school today."

Jaden gave a wide-eyed nod. His chubby fingers clutched his booster seat as I moved us back into the garage. At six, his curly black hair and blue eyes echoed his father. A shiver went through my chest. I would've mistaken it for memories if not for its transformation into spiderwebbing pain. Running to the bathroom, I threw open the toilet lid and knelt over the bowl. A hand patted me on the back. I wiped my mouth and looked. Jaden stood over me, smiling.

"It's okay, Mommy. I'll make some tea."

"Thank you, baby." I staggered to my feet. Going to the garage, I shut the door. As it rolled down, my eyes drifted to the island. It was covered with onion skin, old newspapers, and bills. Some paid, others not so much. One caught my eye. It wasn't a bill; it was a letter. The "From" section made me pause. It read 'Child Protective Services.' Hands twitching, I opened it. Time felt still as I read over the tiny, clinical words. Once done, I lifted my hands to my face. The words were full of legalese, but the intent was clear.

Jaden had missed too much school. Shaking, I picked up my phone. Dialing my mother, I begged her to come over. I had to get Jaden to school. Then I had to talk to my doctor. Forty-five minutes later, Jaden was signed in late at the front office. It took fifteen minutes for Marge to arrive, fifteen more minutes for her to explain how right she was, and finally fifteen more for all three of us to get to his school. Mother— Marge— had never liked Trent. When I started dating him, she'd sighed, clucked her tongue, and muttered how *that boy was going to be trouble.* This was her mantra when we'd become engaged, gotten married, and finally, when he'd walked out in the middle of the night three months ago.

By the time we stopped at the doctor's office, I'd quit responding to her jabs. I pushed open the car door and walked toward the building. Once inside I waved at Tasha. She frowned.

"I thought your appointment was next week."

I scratched the back of my neck. "I need to talk to Dr. Alverez."

"He's in the middle of an appointment."

"Please, I just need a moment," I begged. "The medicine—"

Tasha pursed her lips and pointed to the waiting room. "I'll let him know you're here. But I can't—"

I thanked her and barreled into the waiting room. Time crawled by. Mom went to do some grocery shopping while I sat and stared at the clock. Soon I found myself fidgeting with my phone, taking some online quiz. I was about to get the result of how old I was according to an algorithm when an ad popped up. It was for some medication. A tacky visual of a frowny face turning into a happy face made me cringe, but the words made me look closer. My ailment was right above that stupid grin.

Try Kurathkatsun for all-natural chronic pain relief! See

results in four days or your money back!

"Who buys this crap?" I murmured, consciously extinguishing my hopeful instinct. Still the name lingered in my mind. Its stay was lengthened when I finally talked to Dr. Alverez.

"How much longer do I need to stay on this medicine?" I asked and explained all the side effects I'd been experiencing. He frowned and began muttering about decreasing the dose or changing it up entirely, but I shook my head.

"I need to be well. And soon."

"Your body needs time to heal. You can't rush the process."

"They're going to take Jaden away!" I blurted.

His eyes widened. I realized my blunder and turned my face away. I murmured some excuse and left the examination room. Footfalls pounded behind, but I continued.

"Mrs. Dayton! Hold on."

I paused and turned back. Alverez gave a sympathetic nod. "I'm sorry."

The second time I saw the advertisement, I didn't hesitate to research it. There were plenty of side effects, but not any more than my normal medication. It was slightly expensive but if it could help, it would be worth it. The call was made, the order shipped. Three days later a package arrived

at my door. I sent Jaden to bed
before I opened the box. I
shivered, taking a sip of coffee as
I peered inside. A red wooden box
gazed up at me. I traced the golden
symbol on the lid, then flipped it
open. A single green glass bottle
glinted among faux silk packaging.
I picked it up and discovered
instructions nestled inside the
hollow.

*Take one half dropper in the
morning and another at night. After
the first four days, increase the
dosage to a full dropper.*

I took a dose. The liquid had
canola oil's consistency and was
flavored like apple cider vinegar
and pickle juice. Shuddering, I
clamped down on the urge to retch
and went to bed. The next day, I

felt fantastic. Unlike every other day, I woke up without pain. Jaden got to school, the laundry got done, dinner got in the oven, and I even got a nap. This new energy, nausea and pain free, lasted for two days.

My dreams were the downside. It was dark in there. I was floating through something navy, warm, sticky. Nothing I'd ever seen before. It was night, but the sky was orange, smoke-filled.

The edge of the water, or whatever it was, sat five or ten yards away. I swam toward it. My arms grew tired, but I never got closer. Muscles aching, I stopped to rest. But instead of floating, I slipped beneath the surface. The

deeper I sank, the warmer I grew.
Soon I was boiling.

I awoke and started coughing
over the bed's side. Nothing came
up, but the medicine's taste
lingered in my throat. Sweat
saturated my clothes and I sat up,
taking in my bedroom. It was two
minutes before my alarm was set to
ring. I slipped into the shower,
trying to shake off the dream.
Still, I had no pain. This prompted
me to keep taking the medicine. The
third day went fine. In fact, it
went better then fine.

I got Jaden to school,
organized the garage, and vacuumed
the living room. And the food, the
food tasted so good. I forgot how
long it had been since a strawberry
had tasted sweet to me. Glancing to

the clock, I was jolted from my reverie when I realized something. I was going to be late to pick up Jaden.

Leaving the strawberry stems on the counter, I rushed out the door to get to Jaden's school. I arrived just in time to pick him up. We ran a few errands before getting home. Upon arriving at the grocery store, Jaden asked: "Didn't we go here yesterday?"

Frowning, I scanned my memories. *Did we need more groceries?* In my mind's eye, I went over our refrigerator's interior. It had been full. I laughed it off as a brain fart and took him back home. As we pushed through the kitchen door, I noticed an odd smell. Jaden darted upstairs and I gave a half-hearted "Homework before TV" as I tried to investigate the odors source. I soon found it. There was a bowl of dark blue ooze sitting on the counter. It reeked of rot and decay. Floating on top were green strawberry stems. Stomach churning, I started towards the bathroom. I stopped myself at the threshold. I was fine. Nothing was the matter. I poured the black ooze down the disposal and ran it. The metallic *cachunk* sound was satisfactory.

It was time to take my medicine. It was the fourth day now, and I took the full dropper. My tongue flicked out as I savored the taste.

"Mom?"

Whirling around, a slight figure flicked on the light. There stood a child. My child. My child Jaden.

"Hey, what's the matter baby?"

"Mom. I had a bad dream."

My eyes flicked to the oven clock. The green haze read 3 AM. *Wasn't it 10 PM just a few minutes ago?*

"Mom?"

"Yea, tell me about your dream."

Jaden's eyes widened. "What's on your lips?"

Reaching a hand up, I patted my mouth. When I pulled away, a residue coated my fingers. Navy

ooze. I chuckled. Jaden stepped
back.

I tried to reassure him. "Oh.
How clumsy of me. Mommy must've
forgotten to wipe her mouth." I
reached up my other hand to wipe
away the ooze. In the microwave's
glass front, I noticed I only
managed to smear it around. For
some reason, it didn't bother me.

"Jaden, would you like a glass
of milk?"

I looked for him, but he was
gone. *Where could he have gone?*
Muttering his name, I padded
upstairs. There should've been a
creak to the stairs, but there was
only a low ring. First door on the
left was his. Setting my finger
pads against the door, I pushed. It

swung open. Jaden hurriedly set something on his nightstand. A phone.

"Hey, what's up baby boy? Isn't it a little late to be making calls?"

A wary look filled his eyes. "I was playing a game."

"Oh? What game?"

"Tic Tac Toe."

"That's a fun one."

Jaden frowned. "Are you okay, Mommy?"

"I'm better than okay." I gave a wide grin. "I'm fantastic."

I gave him a kiss on the forehead. From the glow of his nightlight I could see the navy mark I left behind. Closing the door behind me, I went to the bathroom. Hot water poured down on me as I stood in the shower. I closed my eyes and focused on the soft embrace of the water. Turning my head down, my mind slipped into dreams. The navy ooze, the shower turned to a boiling point. I smiled and let myself sink deeper into the pool's embrace.

I woke up, sputtering and coughing. At some point the shower had turned off, but that didn't mean the tub wasn't full. The ooze surrounded me, infiltrated me. I sat up. Through the curtains I could tell it was day. I stood and immediately fell out of the tub. Pulling my way across the tile, I looked back at my legs. They were

swollen, veins visible to bursting.
I pressed a fingertip into my shin.
No sensation accompanied the
puckering of flesh. I crawled from
the bathroom and into the hall.
Through the darkness, I saw that
the first door on the left of the
stairs was open.

"J-Jaden!"

I inched to the threshold and
looked inside. Drawers were flung
open, clothes scattered on the
floor. From my position, I could
see that his adorable suitcase, the
one with the puppy on the front,
was gone. I ground my teeth.

"Mother. That's who the little
rat called."

A chill licked my bare skin. I
reached up and snagged Jaden's

comforter. I wrapped it around myself, letting my eyes flick closed again. I was submerged now, rapidly descending. I breathed in deep for the first time. The ooze slid into my lungs. Cold apathy slid over me as I rolled to my stomach. It lingered as I looked into what lay below. Two eyes, crocodilian, three times my height and ten times my width, returned my gaze.

It studied me for the longest time. Then, in the darkness, something opened below the eyes— a mouth with jagged white fangs. A tongue, along with words, flicked out.

"Come to me child and feel no more pain."

I woke. It was night again. A cool breeze curled through the room. Shadows danced on the ceiling. I tried sitting, only to be punished for it. My abdominals, along with my legs and arms, surged with a thousand pinpricks. With gritted teeth, I forced myself up. My arms dangled against my sides. Breathing heavy, I rested from the exertion. Sleep had almost claimed me again when I heard a sharp creak on the stairs.

Blood pounded in my ears. I tried calling out, but my tongue felt thick, heavy. Another creak erupted. This time it was close to Jaden's room. It was too heavy to be anyone I knew. And it wasn't heavy enough to be anyone I'd

known. Still, I called out his
name.

"Phrenfth?" *Trent?*

The visitor now stood, framed
by the doorway. It wasn't Trent. Or
anyone else I knew. It was tall,
but hunched, with a skeletal
structure, except for its stomach.
This was distended and covered with
gray rotting flesh. A leather belt
hung at its waist, adorned with a
rusty cleaver. Vacancy lived in its
green, Cheshire expression. This
stayed even as it noticed me. It
strode over and sat on the bed next
to me.

"Have you seen him?" It asked.

Dumbfounded, I could not
answer. It repeated the question
and this time I knew what he meant.

The eyes in the depths. I nodded. The vacancy left. It scooped me up as if I was a child and carried me downstairs. I would've struggled, but my arms and legs refused their function. Marching toward the island, he swept bills and onion skins onto the floor. A scream warbled from my throat as he pulled the cleaver from his belt. I tried to move but my body wouldn't obey. The blade came down.

I didn't feel the pain, but my upper arm grew colder as I watched the creature bite down on my forearm. Red trickled down it's chin. Life stirred in its eyes.

"I can see him!" It hissed to someone not there.

I should be passing out. I shouldn't be able to watch, but my brain refused to let me sleep for the first time in a week. He picked up the cleaver again. I closed my eyes, trying to will myself to oblivion, when I heard the door open.

"Mrs. Day—Drop the knife and step away from her!" Someone screeched.

I tried to roll my head toward the newcomer, but the oblivion I asked for arrived. As I drifted, a gun fired. Low ringing filled my ears. Despite trying to stay awake, to see what happened, I fell back into the navy ooze. Many days were spent floating between the surface and wakefulness. After everything, I was no longer surprised. At

least, for the time in my
subconscious. While waking, I was
in a white room. It smelled
sterile. I hated those times. I
hurt so much.

But that time lengthened until
I spent all my time there. Jaden
was sometimes there, so was my
Mother. Occasionally, men in
uniforms stood there. They spoke to
my nurses. My nurses. That's right.
I'm in a hospital. Finally, the day
came where I was lucid. The
detectives entered my room and
asked if they could *have a chat.* I
nodded. Situating themselves on
chairs to either side of me, the
woman began to speak.

"Mrs. Dayton, I'm Detective
Reynolds. This is my associate—"
she gestured to the man with her,

"—Detective Barkley. I know you've been through a lot, but we have a few questions."

I nodded, trying to ignore the nothingness at the end of my left arm. She pulled out a photograph. It was grainy, but I could make out the subject. He was middle-aged, red hair thinning at the top, with a bulbous nose and pale eyes. I frowned.

"I've seen him—I think."

"Can you remember where?" Barkley asked.

Skimming the haze which was my memory over the past few weeks I remembered a uniform and a clipboard.

"He was a delivery man. The one who delivered my medicine."

When Reynolds asked for elaboration, I slowly pieced together what happened. Sympathy, like Doctor Alverez's, circulated in her expression. Barkley took down notes and occasionally asked me to clarify a detail. Once finished, I leaned back against the headrest and realized how foolish I'd been. This epiphany concreted once the officer explained the man's identity.

"Have you heard of the serial killer called The Butcher?"

"No, I try not to pay attention to the news," I explained.

"Fair enough. I ask because this man"— she pointed to the photo—"he is The Butcher."

"He is—" I swallowed. My chest tightened and I was unable to continue. Reynolds told me a little information, enough to inform me without frightening me any further. At least, this was her intent. With a name like *The Butcher*, elaboration wasn't required. More information only added to the terror. The Butcher—his real name was Victor Selk— was like a fisherman who put out many poles. Advertisements for miracle cures were the lures, addresses and credit card information were the hook and line. He'd caught many like me.

"The doctors found an opioid derivative in your system. It matched samples from the other…victims." Reynolds gave a little nod. "We'll nail him with that."

Barkley chimed in. "He calls it his 'tenderizer.' Lets it soften people up for a few days. You should be fine though. Most of it has passed through your system."

I shuddered, but the implications popped up in my mind. "He calls it—you mean you've spoken with him?"

Reynolds smiled. "We have him in custody. It's over."

"You really should thank your kid." Barkley added. "He's the one who called in the first place."

"Jaden called you?" I asked. I was half astonishment and half pride.

Reynolds confirmed her partner's words. "He was worried about you. He thought you were sick."

A smile crossed my face for the first time in a while. My eyes soon wandered down to my new stub. Selk's words came to me. *I can see him.*

The words left my mouth before I could stop them. "I wonder what he meant."

"Sorry?" Reynolds frowned. "What Jaden meant?"

"No—Selk said something. Right before you guys came in." I

elaborated on what little I could
remember.

The two detectives seemed
troubled by this information.
Leaving me for a moment, they
whispered in the corner. I caught
the words *accomplice* and *insanity
plea*. However, my mind soon
returned to Selk's words. They
turned over and over in my head.
Why was he excited to see what I
assume was the same creature from
my nightmares?

*Come to me child and feel no
more pain.*

Those words echoed in my ears
and stamped themselves on my being.
I heard them through the trial.
They magnified as I entered the
witness stand and faced down the

man who ate my hand in front of me.
Selk's grin could've rivaled a
crescent moon.

"I saw him because of you!" He
rejoiced when I testified.

Eventually, he had to be
removed from the courtroom. I
didn't understand what he wanted.
At least, until I realized I'd
stopped having those dreams. In
fact, I stopped dreaming at all.
There was a vacancy where the being
had been. And once I noticed it, I
couldn't stop thinking about it.
Agitation stalked me. Sunlight
blinded me. I stubbed my toe in the
morning and still felt the blow at
night. Then came the cold sweats
and joint aches. And the auditory
hallucinations. Every time I closed
my eyes, I willed the ooze to

surround me. To sink into its warmth— the heat which could turn my bones to jelly—was what I desired above all. Dr. Alverez said I may be experiencing withdrawal from the opioid, but it's been nearly a year since my arm was taken.

After an incident two days ago, a psychiatric ward became my only option. Jaden was home from school, and I was trying to make the house somewhat presentable. Hands shaking violently, I placed the dry dishes in the cupboard. It worsened as I picked up a cheap wine glass. My fingertips left foggy traces on the clear surface. I firmed my grip, trying to steady myself. It shattered. Glass scattered like snow over the

counter and tile floor. I scurried
to the pantry. One hand was on the
broom when a yelp came from the
kitchen. Peering back, I saw Jaden.
He'd stumbled, barefoot, onto the
tile. A large shard was embedded
into his foot. What came from the
injury broke me. Navy ooze dribbled
from his sole onto the floor.

From somewhere in my brain,
arose seven words, ones I hadn't
heard before.

You know how to see me again.

A TARANTISM OF KNUCKLEBONES

Ignore the mud in your sole,
look past aches

in your calves. It's an Orphic
tella we fulfill. So keep

feet light, and missteps
away, for although Death awaits,
Ammit is salivating.

IT'S A GAMBLER'S CITY

T here is this old joke my Dad liked: "How do you get a small fortune?"

I'd always ask *how* even though I'd heard the joke twenty times before. He'd get a little smile and say, "Start with a large fortune and go to Las Vegas."

We'd both chuckle awkwardly and go back to work. Now that I'm in Vegas, a new joke has been added to my repertoire. It's not a funny one. "How do you end up with your ribs cracked in a back alley? Start with a small fortune in Las Vegas and end up borrowing from Billy Mercedes."

Dragging myself from the puddle, I set my back against a graffitied brick wall. My new shoes and the sweater my mom got me for Christmas were ruined. The shoes were a loss I regretted. The sweater? Not so much. The taste of iron settled on my lips as I looked up at Mercedes himself. He was a scrawny guy, with thick glasses and early onset balding. More like an accountant than a Loan Shark. However, he was bookended by two mammoths wrapped in tatts. Mammoths who'd had no trouble pushing me around a second ago.

I braced against the wall and slid to my feet. "Hey Billy."

"The use of my first name is retracted for debtors," he monotoned.

Deciding now wasn't the time to be quippy, I raised my hands in surrender and gave my best apology face. "Alright, Mr. Mercedes. Look. I'll get you your money. Honest. Give me a month—"

"A month?" He exchanged glances with his entourage, then looked back to me. "This is not the time to be trying your failed comedy act."

"Fine. How about a week?" I haggled, trying to read Mercedes' face.

He must kill it at poker. The very game which got me into this mess in the first place. I came to

Vegas the same way every moron
does: by wanting to be successful
at something. What it was I can't
remember. I did find out I was
pretty good at cards. I caught on
to tells fairly quickly, learned
how to be stone-faced, and life was
good. Until Lady Luck decided I
wasn't her favorite anymore. She
picked the best moment to do it
too. High stakes poker game about a
month ago. Wiped me out. Of course,
moron I am, I thought I just had a
bad night. So, I borrowed a little
from Mercedes. The bad night
counter didn't stop at just one. Or
two. Or three.

Mercedes seemed to think about
it a second, then nodded. His eyes
slid once again to his entourage.
"Take a pinky."

Before his words registered, mammoth number one had me in a headlock with my hand against the wall. Mammoth number two pulled a knife. For a solid minute I sputtered out all the pleas I could. Mercedes shook his head and replied. "It's more memorable than a Post-it note."

My scream echoed through the alley. It was muted by the traffic nearby. They dropped me. I heard Mercedes walk away. His voice stayed with me. "See you in a week."

I stayed on the ground. My mind scrambled for a way to pay off the debt. By the time I pulled myself up, I'd decided to run back home. Then I realized I didn't even have the money for a bus ticket. I was about ready to punch the wall when a voice called out to me.

"Having trouble there?"

Glancing to the side I saw a woman. By how tight and low-cut her dress was, when considering the neighborhood, I figured she was a hooker.

"Beat it," I snapped, pulling an old napkin from my coat pocket. I wrapped it around the bloody stump where my pinky used to be. "I ain't in the mood for company."

"I wasn't offering any." She gave me an annoyed look. "But I did overhear your little…disagreement with Mr. Mercedes. How much are you in for?"

When I asked what it mattered

to her, she shrugged and replied, "I know where you can get fast cash, that's all. Five hundred tonight."

I started laughing. "I don't think I look good in underwear, or out of it for that matter."

Her mouth puckered for a moment. "All you'd do is give blood."

I was about to walk away. I wasn't about to fall for some con. I'd probably end up south of the border selling crack or in an ice bath with my kidneys missing, or worse, not waking up at all. But then I saw my paper-wrapped stump. Mercedes was right. It was better than a Post-it note. I sighed and asked what she meant. Her smile grew broader, unnaturally bright in the neon, as she began. There was this clinic five blocks from where we were. All I had to do was follow her there. Then they'd take a little blood, I'd get paid, and then I could go. Every part of my brain except one waved red flags at me, screaming this was a bad idea. But the holdout looked down at my stump. If I didn't produce the money, I was dead anyway. What did I have to lose?

I followed her those five blocks. With everyone I passed I almost backed out. I almost said, *screw it* and left. But still, her swaying hips guided me toward what was presumably the 'clinic.' It looked more like a warehouse, but then again, this operation probably wasn't anywhere near kosher. She stepped up to a side door. Rain misted down. I shuddered. This was my last chance to leave. But I let it slip by as a smaller door opened about eye level. A pale and drawn face appeared at the new vacancy.

My guide spoke. "Hey, it's Sheila. I'm here for my appointment."

"Who's that?"

"A…friend."

The door screeched open and the bouncer waved us inside. I don't know what I expected, but it wasn't what I saw. White tiled floor, bleach white walls, with a little waiting room. I blinked a few times to make sure I wasn't dreaming. Maybe I was. Sheila

called me from the seating area.
She'd casually crossed her legs and
picked up the newest issue of
Vogue. An insistent look got me
next to her. As I settled down, the
doorman, now revealed to be wearing
clean, but faded scrubs, stepped
back behind the counter.

"What is this place?" I
murmured.

"A clinic. Duh."

I was done asking questions. I
hadn't been stabbed at this point,
so I figured I shouldn't try to
prod the lion. Ten minutes later,
the nurse sauntered over and handed
me a clipboard.

"Answer the questions
truthfully and sign"—he pointed to
the bottom of a form attached to

the clipboard—"here."

A prominent black line stood under one clause. *I swear that, to the best of my ability, I will not reveal, hint or imply the location, existence, or activities therein of the Vendsang Clinic.*

Figuring I had no reason not to, I signed my name after answering the questionnaire. No history of mental illness, some heart trouble on my mom's side, and I had a pollen allergy. Once done, I handed the clipboard to the nurse. He in turn took it through a door behind him. Hardly a minute passed before a doctor stepped into the lobby. I assumed she was a doctor by the authority with which she walked, rather than any name tag. The white lab coat helped the notion. She was grayed, in her mid-sixties, with a slight but permanent hunch to her shoulders. A curdled look went through her dark green eyes upon seeing me.

"Sheila. Why is this person here?"

Sheila scratched her neck and gave a cheeky grin. "I needed some extra cash and figured there would be a referral bonus?"

Judging by the doctor's face, this was not the right answer. Still, the older woman sighed and looked to me. "Second door on the left."

I gave a quick nod and hurried past. I didn't want to be in the middle of that argument. However, I did catch something the doctor said just before I entered my room.

"Let's talk in my office."

The door clicked shut behind me and again I was surprised at how normal everything was. There was the odd gray, padded but still uncomfortable chair. One with the bar that slides down in front of you. Inside stood a heavy-set woman in scrubs, her hair up in a messy bun. What followed was so standard and by the book there was an absurdity to it. The tourniquet, the needle going in, red ichor flowing through a tiny tube. The only difference was at the end, instead of me forking over cash, I was handed five one-hundred-dollar bills. Sheila told the truth. I stepped from the room, hoping to find her. It didn't take me long.

Two men walked away, each holding two corners of a blue plastic tarp.

My eyes widened when I saw what they carried atop it. Sheila. Her body jerked with the heavy lurching of the men's movements. She was pale, exposed eyes rolled back, with her veins darker, more pronounced. What I noticed first was the gaping, yet somehow bloodless, hole in her throat. By the time this registered, the two men had ducked into another door. I ran over and jerked at the door. It was locked.

My fist slammed into the frame as I demanded entry. However, a coughing from behind soon stopped me. It was the old woman. Her white lab coat was gone, but red splattered her worn button-down shirt. She was holding a handkerchief, also stained, to her mouth. The word *vampire* stumbled out of my mouth before I could stop it.

"I suppose I am." She tucked her hanky into her pants pocket. "Still, if you think that makes Sheila the victim in this case, you are sorely mistaken."

It took me a few minutes to find my voice. "What do you mean?"

"The problem with this town is there are one too many gamblers. No one is content with what they have."

There was an itch in my soul, as if she somehow knew why I was here in the first place. I then remembered my bloody stump. As I slid my hand into my pocket, she gave a dry chuckle.

"Don't worry, I couldn't run a place like this if I couldn't control myself." Her expression grew darker. "I also can't run it if people are constantly bringing in 'referrals.'"

When her meaning dawned on me, a cold sensation fell over me. A question came to mind.

"What will you do with me?"

A predatory look entered her eyes. "You signed the contract. Just don't break one rule."

None of the nurses tried to stop me, and I didn't stay long. I staggered down the road, feeling the bills in my pocket. I wanted to get as far away as possible. I wanted to forget everything. Rain quickly soaked my shoes. And the rest of me. Forcing the clinic from my mind, I ducked into the nearest building. I shuddered and shook off the excess water. Bright lights flooded my vision. Cigar smoke floated through the air, and glasses clinked at a nearby bar. When my eyes looked deeper into the building, I noticed the stuffed booths, sticky carpeting, laughter, shuffling cards and the cranking of slot machines.

I'd wandered into a casino.

And I'd taken three steps toward the poker tables. *What am I doing?* Taking a few deep breaths, I closed up my coat and turned to leave. An alarm went off. A very familiar one.

Someone had won. Someone had won. Sweat beaded on my brow. I could stay a little while longer. After all, it was raining outside.

CURIO

Leather-skinned lady, did they take your emerald
eyes and give you obsidian? It's hard
to tell out here beyond glass, within
must of decaying treasure-trash.

Newspaper sits to your left, five
grand of *Dear Emily* gathering
dust next to a carpet bag holding
Faberge remains. If you look

close, green bottles of hens'
teeth and monkey brains observe
those who pass on blue
sugar crystals on tiny
posts.

HOIA-BACIU

I'm in purgatory I suppose. Though, I don't know when it started. Or when it might end. Every day I travel—traveled—travel these same woods alongside many others. Soft grass tickles our feet, breezes caress our skin. We walk together, and yet alone. There used to be so many of us. Hundreds, thousands even. We'd walk in silence, for this was our way. To be a figment was our nature, and in nature we remained. It was naïve to think this would last.

Every day I am followed, in the same way my fellows are.

Crunching boots and heavy breathing seek us. They are from the same people, or at least, similar people. Their faces blur. Sometimes they are old, sometimes they are young. In the beginning we spotted lone travelers, single torches, and *who's there*. In as many ways they changed; they stayed the same. They now bring equipment in big black vans, the ones with the sliding side doors. As if they're an undercover SWAT team. At least, that's what the younger of us say they look like. I wish I could leave this place, or at least have new people to walk alongside me. The more often these intruders come, the more often my fellows simply cease. Like Robert.

Many months ago, Robert was taken by the men in the black van.

As the oldest, his loss stung us. A young one said they watched the scene, unable to help. Robert was on his normal evening walk when they came across him. Their bright lights shown in his face. When he begged them to leave him be, they laughed. Among their screeches, one shouted: "We have an EVP! We have an EVP!"

They pointed things at him, clicking punctuated his cries. Soon he was gone. Taken into their machines. Robert wasn't the first to go. He also wasn't the last. Now, quite alone, I am on my normal walk. My fellows are gone; Jasmine, Brody, Heather, countless others. The men, their numbers increased, come by more often now. Will their hunger never be satisfied?

I stop suddenly, realizing my

usual following is not the usual suspects. Easing behind a tree, I watch them. My fingers curl against the bark and my lips press tight. I don't silence my breathing. I haven't breathed in a long time. They stumble around, glowing machines in hand. Their clicking machines are ready to take me away. They pass. I note their number. Ten. When the last one hikes past, I close my eyes and let myself devolve.

My skin becomes ashen, nails harden and grow sharp. My eyes slide open, tongue flicks over rotted teeth. Silent as the grave and carrying her message I follow the last one; a red-headed man with a patchy beard. As my teeth dig into his neck, my hand clamps over his mouth. I am the last image he

will receive. And in seeing me, he
got what he came for.

COMPOSTING

If nothing, I am
a turnip. Though I never became
the new moon I was promised,
sand still flows from
one glass cone to the next. I often
wonder if in my quest
to twitch light I bred
blasted heaths. To see the guts,
the box; to awaken the *behelit*
I was never given. My life
feels like it was quasi: old ambition
leaking from new wineskins. Hunger
blinds to wax—
nature. Gnawing flesh,
Romero's sons rending
marrow from bone, drive from
the engine. I bite into

a rotten apple; proving myself to the maggots, vultures and
a confident philosopher, I can see the construction begin on
thank you. But I can't help but notice my
lackluster ideas that have no market value. I travel via
beg to be the ground floor when I find I'm already there.
I'll find the albatross on land. In my failings
finger paintings and paper hand turkeys resurrected rather than
the coal powered steam drive: I should've read outside
and rocked him back to sleep. This was a chance that
always reenters the riptide. This patchwork
bests and raises the ancient compassion
and complacency
molds the ore to its own
infernal sleeping. Auntie Misery is soon keeping
sinew from muscle. But I go deeper, dividing
passion. I don't want to stay by
nothing—

MEN AT WORK

I wouldn't be here if not for Jeremy. More specifically, how Jeremy looked. Six-foot, strong jaw, and eyes dreamy enough to make me forget he was covered with sawdust. I guess I'm pretty shallow like that. Maybe if I was less shallow, I wouldn't be here now.

I met Jeremy through my job, sort of. I worked retail in an older building, where a bunch of different shops are on the first floor and offices are on the upper ones. It was and still is undergoing construction. How long has the work been going on? Months?

Years? Decades? I can't tell anymore. While I was there, the building was non-smoking, but for three days tobacco scented the interior. On the fourth day, I'd had enough. Leaving the store— what type of store was it? I can't remember. Anyways, I marched out the door toward the construction guys on break. I was going to give them Hell. But of course, I saw Jeremy and well, it was less hell I was spitting and more strong suggestions.

He got the other guys to put out their cigs and I noticed he had two tattoos. One on each shoulder. A bird was on the left: a testament to his mom. She'd died while serving in the Air Force. A tree was on the right. The way its thin branches twisted revealed a skull.

He'd survived OD'ing right out of high school. I'd learned this over dinner and drinks the following weekend, and we swapped numbers. I had a good time, and I was pretty sure he did too.

But the next week, he wasn't at the site. Looking back, none of the original crew was there. I tried to ask one guy, but he murmured that the previous groups contract had "fallen through."

I would've pushed it, but there was something off about these guys. For one, their eyes were...trippy. You know, they looked like they'd smoked a blunt. Their pupils were always dilated and when they talked to you, they looked toward you, but never looked at you. Their foreman was the worst. From his appearance, I'd say

his last bath was at the first
Woodstock. Yellowed rotten teeth
protruded from his gums and when he
spoke to me, I grew nauseated from
his breath.

'Why don't you call him
instead of interrupting our work?"

After the look he gave me, I
decided to stop asking. His eyes
were a reversal of the crew. Almost
too aware, as if he could look at a
person and correctly guess their
heartbeat. I took his advice and
called Jeremy.

I decided I wasn't going to be
"that" girl, the type who called
seven times in five minutes. So, I
left a quick text and waited a few
days. Nothing. I decided to call
one more time, and if there was no
response, I'd take the hint. The
phone did its normal thing, buzzing

a few times. My feet tapped and I
leaned against the brick wall of
the building. Bored, my focus went
toward 'the box'. One of the
renovations involved installing a
central elevator. For safety
purposes, four plywood walls were
erected around the construction
zone. It was padlocked as well, and
despite everyone who came and left
the box, I'd never seen the
interior. For months, all sorts of
noises came out of there. One day
they spent two solid hours
jackhammering the old concrete
floor. I went home with a migraine
that day.

The phone stopped buzzing and
I was told by a cheery robot voice
that this number's voicemail was
full. I hung up. It should've been
the end of the story. If I hadn't

left my phone inside the store. I
was halfway home before I realized
it was missing. It was eleven, and
I wanted to go home, but I didn't
like the guy who opened the next
day. Sighing, I turned the car
around and went back. It was dark
inside, but not as dark as it
should've been. Light poured from
the ventilation holes in the box.
At first, I figured it was a night
shift. But, as I took a few steps
toward my storefront, I realized
the noises coming from inside those
plywood walls weren't the thuds of
hammers. They were voices. Not
speaking but chanting. I decided
the phone could wait and turned
toward the exit. My way to the
glass-paneled door was blocked.
Basking in the moonlight was a
cloaked figure, its eyes gleaming a

soft purple. It was the foreman. Something heavy came down on my head and I blacked out.

I woke up here. It's been a while since someone else was thrown down the elevator shaft. First came the original crew, then a homeless man or two, then me, and then you. I don't know why I'm saying this. You probably can't understand me. See, what we're floating in is stomach acid. His stomach acid. Those men, the ones pretending to be construction workers, call him Kurathka-Tsun, the great eater. They're idiots of course. This thing is far older, fouler. I know because each day I become more and more a part of him. I'm not even sure if you can understand me. In the end Jeremy couldn't form words and, in the beginning, I only recognized him by his tattoos. He just sounded like a rasp, a hiss, a dead thing.

Even if you can't understand me, I could help you. There is a chance. One of the homeless men found a passageway. It opened when pushed in a particular way. I may have enough strength—my muscles are still partially there, though I can see my bones. I could help. I could help.

But I don't want to die alone.

MISS THE MOTHER

Start as all women do: Maid
of youth. One eye between
a hero's thumb and pointer. Tooth
shuffled among three. Toil
and bubble given throughout the
scene.

Improvised but outlined, guide
Macbeth, Perseus, but we
remain in limbo until the finale.

Then we're left as the Crone.

EYES

Not sure how to begin exactly. I guess I should start with Mr. Sprinkles. No, I didn't name him that, I actually wanted to name him Slash. He's a long-haired black cat and my Dad was a big Guns and Roses fan. But Mr. Sprinkles was a rescue and he refuses to respond to his new name. I mean, he refused. Stupid cat. I got him because I didn't want to come home to an empty apartment. Ever since then, he was a real pain. Toys I picked for him were ignored in favor of socks, remotes, and a necklace my grandmother got me two years ago. He also knew the best places to get stuck. One day, I came home from work to find him upside down, his head caught between the thin metal bars of my towel rack. Half an hour and many clawings later, he was free. However, I wasn't entirely blameless in our relationship's dysfunction.

Right after I got him, my new job turned out to have a lot more travel time than I thought. Normally, I had a few days a week where I'll get home after ten. This worked and allowed me time to play with him. But my promised hours weren't upheld. Nights grew later and later. This last week was awful. Mornings found me rushing out and I would stagger back after 11 PM. By then I just wanted to crash. I felt bad for Mr. Sprinkles. I didn't even see him most days, except a tail's flick or eyes' glimmer.

It wasn't just me who felt bad for him. My neighbor, Ms. Allen, expressed her concern. It was almost a ritual for her. She'd start her day with 6 AM gardening. I knew this because she told me: "If I can get up at six in the morning to garden, surely you can get up half an hour earlier and play with that poor creature."

At first I would chuckle, hiding my annoyance, and go on my way. As the weeks dragged on, however, I began to ignore her. Mr. Sprinkles seemed to be judging me too. I'd stagger in and be greeted by his green eyes glowing in the dark. Last month had been murder on the electric bill, so I'd leave the lights off. I could make my way through the dark.

My boss said my hours would revert after this current week, so I promised myself I would get him a new toy, or some treats to make up for my crappy cat parenting. On the final long night, I flopped into bed as normal, making a mental note to hit the pet store tomorrow. And change the litter box. The smell from the bathroom was awful.

Flicking off the lights, I turned to my side, and listened to the rain outside. I don't know what woke me, maybe the lightning outside, maybe some crash from a neighboring unit, but I sat up and listened, scanning the room for an intruder. The mattress springs creaked as something darted off the bed. Green eyes flicked my way in the dark before disappearing from the room.

A part of me was weirded out by how loud the creak was. Like something heavier than a cat had tumbled from the bed. But I was tired and decided to leave any investigation for the morning. The eyes were obviously Mr. Sprinkles. He'd probably just gained a little weight. At least, that's how I convinced myself to go back to sleep.

The next morning, I decided to clean the litter box first. As I stepped into the bathroom, bile crept up in my throat. The smell was stronger, and different. Like spoiled meat. Mr. Sprinkles must've caught a mouse and buried it in the box. My hands shook as I lifted the top of the litter box. A scream caught in my teeth as I fell into the bathtub. An animal was inside, but it wasn't a mouse. The body of a long-haired black cat lay curled among the litter. Maggots writhed in the bloody stump where its head should've been.

He had been dead for several days.

THE MODERN PROMETHEUS 2.0

I did not want to build you
from criminal clay, so I (in my quiet

haste) replaced Ygor with Sandman:
corporeal
for discarnate.   Is this how
a widow feels   sending her
Spartan

off?   The inkling
by pulling the switch, letting
blue light twitch   through you, I

set expiration dates. I'm tired,
but I sit by you and wait
for a lightning strike.

DAILY GRINDS

B eing a witch wasn't a requirement for working at the Weird Sisters Café, but it sure helped one get hired. However, Malcolm MacCowl, the owner's son, didn't have a lick of magic in him. A fact he was now explaining nervously, to his friend and co-worker Didya.

"Ha! I always knew it." Her gray eyes shifted green, a sign of her newest experiment.

"You—Who told you?" Malcolm stammered, heated.

Instead of answering, Didya turned to the espresso machine. Her loose dreads, partially bound in a colorful scarf, swerved in her wake. Her complexion was the same color as her objective: a second—no third Americano. It had been a slow day, and she'd decided it was time to try new flavors. When the beans began to grind, Malcolm tried a different question.

"How have you not had a heart attack yet?"

She gestured to her eyes, now a deep pink. "Something not far off from these bad boys."

Recovered from his embarrassment, Malcolm frowned. "What do mood eyes have to do with your caffeine addiction?"

"They're both simple transmutes, Boo. Homeschooling got you nowhere. Didn't Mr. Midas even teach you theory?"

When Malcolm hit sixth grade, he was swiftly pulled from school. Along with acne and odd smells, magic accompanied puberty for all his friends. He'd just gotten the blackheads. And lost touch with the kids he knew. He'd only run into Didya again when she applied for a job at the Weird Sisters freshman year. Except for dreads and magic, she hadn't changed much. Once the hot water had run its course, Didya poured espresso over into a plastic cup set upon the worn smooth wooden counter. The ice inside soon melted. With the grounds from the portafilter in the trash, she looked to Malcolm.

"What should I try?"

Malcolm shrugged. "Uh, Bacon?

She raised a dark brow. "And I thought I was the basic one."

"Well—bacon tastes…good." Malcolm shrugged. "Besides, the last time you tried savory was months ago."

"And with good reason. Mushroom was a crap idea." Didya cracked her neck. "Fine then, let's try bacon."

She stood still, and it was obvious she was waiting for something. It took a second for it to sink in, but Malcolm got the hint. Stretching his scrawny six-foot frame, he gripped the simple syrup on the top shelf. Looking down at her, he chuckled. "Thought you were going to use a simple levitation. I would've figured that would've been the first thing you learned. With shelves and all."

Didya hadn't changed much. That included her height. Her frame had grown to five-foot and decided to call it quits. Her eyes widened at his remark, but soon her orange-painted lips widened into a grin.

"Wow. I'm about as roasted as the coffee." She rolled her still pink eyes. "In my defense, it's easier to change something than fight gravity."

Taking the syrup from him, she poured a small amount of the thick, sticky liquid into a clean espresso cup. Carefully, she replaced the cap before handing it back to Malcolm. Without need for instruction, he returned it to the top shelf. The last time they'd done savory, the spell had caught all the simple syrup batch. In the end, they'd had a near full bottle of sticky mushroom ooze.

After a brief panic, they told Midas MacCowl what happened.

Oddly enough, Malcolm's father hadn't been especially mad. Except for the fact they'd wasted the full bottle. He made a deal with them where they could continue experimenting if they told him which flavors worked. And if they were more cautious in the future.

Didya prepared the spell,

placing the espresso cup in a busted microwave. This in turn was set on a heavy oak table in the industrial-vibed dining area. If there was an explosion, at least it would be somewhat contained. Unlike the first time they'd tried this. Malcolm pulled out their trial list; a simple table with flavors on one side and the result on the other. It was on a notepad hidden beneath the espresso machine. Brown splotches and grounds covered it, but he could still read the blurred letters. Most flavors ended up duds, but there were a few exceptions: Caramel Corn, Peanut Brittle, Moose Tracks, Cucumber Sandwich, Lemongrass, and, surprisingly, Steak.

Reaching her hand into the

microwave, Didya dipped her fingertip into the syrup. She hummed. Air around her seemed to thicken, fade, and concentrate around the espresso cup. Removing her hand, she shut the door and took a few steps back. Her eyes shifted to gray as words tumbled free.

"Sutluts Sutualp te."

When the last word ended, the cup rattled inside the microwave. The yellow light blanketing the café faded in and out as energy thickened the air. Panic slipped over Didya's face as her dreads lifted. Malcolm got ready to grab her and pull her behind the counter. The fogged door opened. Nothing terrible sprung out. With caution they approached their experiment. The syrup had turned opaque gray and now had a booger's consistency. Didya's upper lip curled.

"Mal. Get your drink ready." She glanced toward him. "I'm not trying *that* alone."

"Didn't plan on backing out now." Malcolm went over and poured himself a cup of regular coffee.

Once he and his drink were near her, Didya separated half the goop into each cup. Together, they stirred. Oddly, the gelatinous nature dissolved with ease. Soon the drinks were ready. The two who were supposed to consume them were not.

Didya's brow furrowed. "Want to get ENS on call?"

"I don't think we're going to need a necromancer." Malcolm responded, his eyes not leaving his drink. "Besides, they charge an arm and a leg for even recent revivals. I don't want to exhume Uncle Matthew again."

"Your dad did say to be careful." Didya pulled out her scryer. It was a flat piece, the consistency of onyx, with a flower etched in the back. Jealousy ate at him as he thought of his own communicator; a plastic hunk the size of a brick with rubbery buttons and terrible reception. The 'telephone', as it was called, was created for Duds like him by some guy named Eddy Sun a few decades back. Trying to banish his envy, he looked at something new— a hole was

drilled in the bottom left corner.
Laced through was a blank-faced
cloth Hoko doll.

Noting this, Malcolm asked;
"Your grandma still wanting
grandkids?"

Didya nodded. "She gets me a
new one every year."

"Sheesh. Has Raj even proposed
yet?"

"It's been pretty quiet on
that front." Didya changed the
subject. "How about you? Any big
news?"

Malcolm followed this new
direction. "Dad's retiring."

"Oh."

"And he wants me to take

over."

"Do you want to?"

Malcolm leaned into the counter and looked at his coffee. It was getting cooler every moment. However, it was going to taste, he knew it would be better warm. "I'll answer after we drink this down."

Sighing, she lifted her cup. "Cheers!"

After he mirrored her gesture, they took a deep gulp. And then another. The worried cynicism on their faces morphed into satisfied grins.

Didya grinned. "Now that's good stuff."

"Agreed. Put another one down for savory?" Malcolm took a swig and grabbed a pencil.

Graphite scratching across the notepad, his brow furrowed. As the last pencil stroke ended, he still had no idea how to tell Didya the full truth. Midas MacCowel wanted the shop to stay in the family, but without magic, there was no way Malcolm could run the Weird Sister. A good chunk of the building maintenance, daily prep, and a thousand other things relied on the owner's ability to do magic. Even his own dumb phone needed someone else to power it in the morning.

"What good is a coffee shop owner who can't even power on an espresso machine?" He muttered, forgetting Didya in his musings.

"A heckin' good one." Didya's

voice cut through the fog. "You crunch numbers and handle shipments. I'll cover the espresso machine."

"Didya—" Malcolm tried to stop her.

"Now of course, this means I'll be co-owner. I'm my own boss."

"Didya—"

"And I get a raise. None of this 'slightly over minimum' mess."

"Didya!"

"What?"

"*This is never going to work. We're going to fail and be homeless and*—Thank you," He smiled.

She finished her drink and returned the smile. "Your welcome.

Now come on. We have a lot to clean
up."

ELEGY FOR THE INFERNAL GOLEM

I shouldn't have broken you into so few
remnants. If you'd been ground,

there'd be new shapes or you
could have been cast

into space to settle. To pull
toward more of the same, a glimmer
reaching back to launch
point. But there is enough

to make out strands
of your hair, Roman slant

of your nose, stains
of your irises. The Sandman (and I) built

you well—Blame wasn't to be found
in you. Mirages
don't catalyze themselves.

DOORKNOBS

I lived in an old house my first year in college. And when I say old, I mean freakin' old. Well over a century and some change. My landlord bought it two years ago, patched some holes, replaced some siding, and whitewashed the interior. I mean, in a house this old, time is bound to do a number on it. Problem is, time wasn't the only one wearing the poor girl down. The structure spent a good ten percent of its life unoccupied, unless you count the hobos who broke in to steal the copper wiring. And the doorknobs.

I mention those last ones because they're why my rent is so cheap. Or at least, was cheap. See, when my landlord was about ready to open the house, he decided to go on a quick weekend getaway to take the edge off. I mean, I get it. He expected a bunch of stoners to show up and fumigate the place the following week. He probably wasn't expecting police cars when he got back. Turns out, the guys who took the knobs before came back to try again. I found out later they'd taken every single one in the house, along with the faceplates.

I had no idea about this when I signed the lease. When you're on a fixed budget in a college town, seeing rent below seven hundred a month is a done deal. Heat doesn't work too well? I'll buy a sweater.

Plumbing is awful? Hey no flooding, no problems.

It was kind of weird how I was the only one there. The house was a duplex. My landlord got the left side and I got the right side. I was told I was going to have a roommate, so I'd asked, jokingly, about this. That was when I found out about the doorknobs. Apparently when the other girl found out about the break in, she'd decided to rent elsewhere. When I looked at the newer doorknobs, I was surprised to find none of them matched. Some were glass, others had a handlebar, others were bronze. When I inspected what was going to be my bedroom, the closet door had a flower detailed on the faceplate. Not quite a rose, maybe a tulip?

"They're here now?" I asked.

He gave a vague reply. "Found used ones online, just in time."

I'd been there a month when weird crap started happening. The landlord didn't smoke, and I'd quit last year, but I'd smelled smoke in the laundry room. Not from cigarettes, but wood smoke. It got so bad one night I nearly hacked up a lung. When the landlord noticed it too, he called in the fire department. They looked around, checking the usual suspects, but in the end, there was nothing. I'd have left, but again, the rent was cheap and Bill, my landlord, was an alright guy. He was older and he'd served in what he called *Nam*. He'd tell you about it too. I'd have gotten annoyed, but he made freakin' good sloppy joes and was crap at cards. Second round of

weird crap started one night after
a poker game with his *Nam* friends.
I'd folded early. Midterms started
that week and I wanted to do some
last-minute cramming. But when I
opened the door, I noticed
something odd. There is a shared
screened-in porch on the back of
the duplex. It's almost like an air
lock. One screen door followed by
the real backdoor. And with the
light from Bill's side, I could
tell that back door was open. By
instinct I stepped back into Bill's
section. My own rinky dink
apartment felt more like the set to
a cheap 80s slasher.

When that comparison came to
mind, I got mad at myself. I'm a
grown woman for cryin' out loud.
But I couldn't help but remember
the break-in. I turned back to the

poker table. Bill had noticed I
wasn't going in and asked what was
going on, I told him about the
door. I tried to laugh it off,
saying a cat must've gotten in, but
Bill shook his head and nodded at
his buddy Theo. They stood from the
table and went to check my side of
the duplex. Terry and Vee stayed
behind to make sure no one cheated.

Later, I'd feel embarrassed at
the messy state of the bathroom,
and the…choice…laundry items left
out, but right then I was relieved
to see Bill and Theo come stomping
back into the room. No one was in
there. Bill told me if anything
like that happened again, I should
call him, and he'd check it out.
Theo cracked a joke about the Hello
Kitty lamp I had upstairs, trying
to lighten the mood. It wasn't

funny, but I laughed anyway, trying to shake off the paranoia.

Bill and I had grown close by that time. His kids lived several states away, and my parents were 'taking some time apart.' That's probably why I tried not to complain. The smoke smell had become a constant and while I never found the outer door open again, I found several doors slightly ajar. I thought it was the stress of the semester until they started slamming.

First time was in the middle of the night the day I came home from spring break. I was up late studying, when a sudden crash rattled the house. Looking to the clock, it read 3 AM. But I picked up the phone to call Bill anyways.

"C'mon, c'mon Bill. Either you

made that racket, or it woke you."

A few minutes later, Bill answered.

"You alright Margot?"

"Yeah. You?"

"Yeah. That was on my side, I think. Stay on the line, I'm going to check."

"Sure."

For a few minutes all I heard was mumbling and creaking stairs. Finally, Bill cussed over the phone. A door he'd left open was shut. This happened a few more times, sometimes in the day, sometimes at night. They were checked a couple times, by Bill's friends, then by an expert. We heard the same old story. Nothing was wrong. Then Bill's sister got sick. She hadn't been feeling well for some time, but her doctor had finally made *that* call. The call no one ever wants to get. Bill said he'd be gone for probably a couple of days, maybe a week. He asked if I would be okay, and I'd laughed.

"C'mon Bill, it's just doors slamming."

Bill shrugged. "Yeah, sure. You're right, kiddo. See you in a few days."

Those first couple nights were fine. The final one hit like a truck. I was browsing the internet, looking for somewhere cheap to go for a day trip, when something caught my attention. Taking out my ear buds, I listened. I was expecting the creak of a door. I found whimpering. It was chilled, child-like, and warped as if it was through water. And it was coming from my closet. No, that wasn't

quite right. It was coming from the
doorknob. My first thought was to
bolt from the room. I slipped out
of bed, letting my feet fall softly
onto the carpet. The sound
continued as I took my first step
forward. With my second, it
stopped. Then came the voice.

"Don't go out there."

Sarcasm must be my fear
response. "Oh, and why not?"

"He'll get you."

The smell of smoke grew
stronger as a chill swept over me.
My eyes went between my exit and my
closet. I knew opening either door
was probably a dumb decision, so I
tried a different tactic. I knelt
by the closet door and peered into
the keyhole. There was little
light, just what came from behind
me, but I could tell two things.

One, what lay before me wasn't my closet. My clothes were gone and in their stead were cardboard boxes. The second thing caught my attention more. There was someone— something more like— in there. Two eyes glimmered in something too wispy to be a silhouette. I staggered back into the bed. My hands shook as I reached for my cell phone. I ended up knocking it off the nightstand. My fingers had just brushed the glass front of the phone when the knob of my bedroom door began to turn.

I threw myself off the bed, body slamming the door and setting my whole frame against it. Still, I felt myself jump forward as what felt like a fist slammed into the door. A voice, rough and heavy, called from the other side of the door. I couldn't make out the words beyond 'Emily' and 'let me in'. I stayed quiet, hoping it would forget the sound of me crashing into the door earlier. It didn't. The fist slammed over and over into the door. With every rattle, the urge to scream grew. And when the screams started, the battering intensified. My pleas for help were short-lived, however. It was becoming hard to breathe. Even looking back now, I don't know why I decided to look through the keyhole. Maybe it was some attempt to find out what was going on. Maybe if I knew what was bombarding my home, I could survive it.

I don't remember passing out, but the EMTs told me I wasn't under long before the fire department kicked down the door. Apparently, the smoke detector had gone off. Odd thing though. There was plenty of smoke, but no fire. No little girl either. No sign of that thing from beyond the keyhole. At this point, the rest of this story was told to me. I was in the hospital when Bill arrived home. I was told Bill was depressed. I was told Bill probably lit the fire in some vague suicide attempt. The fire that consumed the duplex the night he got home. After all, his sister had just died. I don't believe a word of it. After what I saw online, I don't know what to think.

"Joseph Fredricks, Serial Killer, Goes by Lethal Injection."

The picture right under the headline stopped my skimming. The face I'd seen beyond the keyhole had been inhuman, twisted, melted,

with a sinister grin. Nightmare
fuel to the max. The face I saw now
was human. But something in the
face, the eyes, the expression,
made me dig through the article.
Fredricks was a serial killer with
a count anywhere between thirteen
and twenty-five. According to law
enforcement officers, it was
difficult to tell because of his
MO.

I dove into the listed
references. Somewhere, there had to
be something. A few hours later,
I'd dug up an address. I didn't
know what I'd find there, besides
an old crime scene, but something
in me said to see this through. I
hit the road after Bill's funeral.
His Nam buddies told me before I
left that I could join them for
next week's poker game. I said sure

even though I was pretty sure I wouldn't be up for it when the time came.

Three hours later, I stood before a black husk of a building. Two crows stared down at me as the orange evening light draped across a collapsed roof. I knew it would be stupid to go in, but I crept up the front steps, testing each one before setting down my full weight. Eventually I stood before the front double doors. I let my fingers brush them, feeling soot powder the tips. Taking a deep breath, I pushed it open. It was stiff, but gradually gave. Pulling out my phone, I let my cell light dance across ash-stained walls and ruined floorboards. But then I saw it.

Fredricks was a serial killer, and his weapon of choice was fire.

It had been hard to tell at first, because the fires were spaced out over a decade, but something did create a pattern. In each case, a doorknob was taken from the home. His collection was never found.

When I went into that house, my light fell upon a storage closet to the left. It was slightly ajar. I could see the crumbling remains of cardboard boxes inside. A cold breeze swept past me as my gaze went to the right. The door to the living room caught my attention, and when the horror of my situation sunk in, I checked every doorknob I could safely maneuver toward. Each one had a flower detailed on the faceplate. Not quite a rose, maybe a tulip.

I've started smoking again.

AND I AM CONTENT.

Truly told, within the conch shell
of my mind resides (with all
the modern luxuries
of course) a little gnomic

man: bespectacled, bewildered,
but brilliant. In retrospect, I
have
no idea how he came to perch upon
my medulla, but there
he speaks and sleeps. Dictating

what simple etchings will travel
from one tip to another. He asks
little
just consistency (in quantity
and quality) in his diet: peach
schnapps and molten

fondue. He never forgets
that without me he has no
arms or legs. Trying to hide

his influence and allowing
the taste of fruit. However,

my prose is not my own. I had
myself surgically
removed—

Originally Published in Dark River
Review

SPECIAL THANKS

Cthulhu R'ley Cthulhu R'ley
Cthulhu R'ley Cthulhu R'leyCthulhu
R'ley Cthulhu R'leyCthulhu R'ley
Cthulhu R'leyCthulhu R'ley Cthulhu
R'ley Cthulhu R'ley Cthulhu R'ley
Cthulhu R'ley Cthulhu R'ley Cthulhu
R'ley Cthulhu R'ley Cthulhu R'ley
Cthulhu R'ley Cthulhu R'ley Cthulhu
R'ley Cthulhu R'ley Cthulhu R'ley
Cthulhu R'ley Cthulhu R'ley Cthulhu
R'ley Cthulhu R'ley Cthulhu R'ley
Cthulhu R'ley-

Just joking. I think it would
be easier to blame this book on
Cthulhu than list everyone who made
this project possible.

But I'll do my darndest.
First off, to everyone who has
supported me via YouTube, Patreon,
or other social media outlets
throughout this endeavor. You guys
rock.

Secondly, to my Mother and
Father. Pop, thanks again for
introducing me to horror. Mom,
thanks for being willing to read my
book, even though I know this isn't
your favorite genre.

Thirdly, I want to thank my
family members. I couldn't have
done this without your love or
support. A special thanks to my
sister Natalie and Brother-in-Law
Austin.
You two played Devil's
Advocate a lot with my writing.

Especially you, Natalie. I hate and love you for it. But thank you for knowing I could do better than the first draft.

Fourthly, a big thanks to all of my friends who listened to me talk about this book without complaining. And for giving me solid advice on how to proceed. Seriously, guys. I must've talked your ear off about this darn thing.

Thank you for enduring the babbling. Especially Julie, the Terry clan, Charles, the Russell duo, and random strangers I run into all the time.

Finally, God. He brought all of these people into my path and he gave me the courage to fight my demons long enough to get this book done.

Here's to the next book.

ABOUT THE AUTHOR

Creepy, Christian, and a Cat Mom, Alyssa Hazel has had a love affair with Horror her entire life. Her work has found homes with the Dark River Review, Red Coyote Review, and Bluestem Magazine. She can be found playing with the monsters under her bed. Or maybe she's just trying to get Tim out from there for the fiftieth time

Made in the USA
Lexington, KY
01 November 2019

56398795R10118